# THE EXPENDABLES

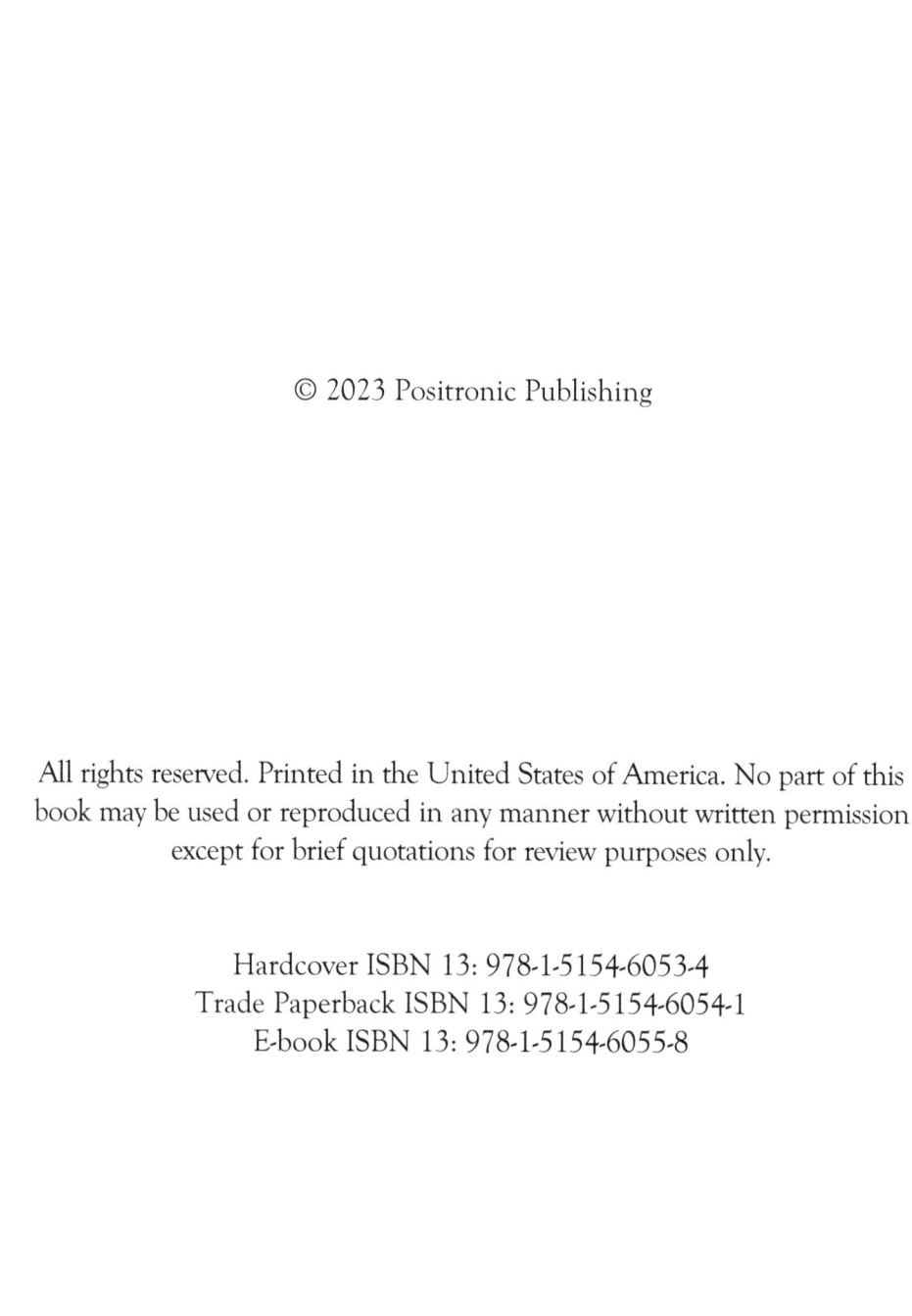

Hardcover ISBN 13: 978-1-5154-6053-4
Trade Paperback ISBN 13: 978-1-5154-6054-1
E-book ISBN 13: 978-1-5154-6055-8

# THE EXPENDABLES

by A. E. Van Vogt

*The alien was deadly, dangerous and inhuman—but he was not the most feared enemy on the ship!*

I

One hundred and nine years after leaving Earth, the spaceship, *Hope of Man*, went into orbit around Alta III.

The following "morning" Captain Browne informed the shipload of fourth and fifth generation colonists that a manned lifeboat would be dropped to the planet's surface.

"Every member of the crew must consider himself expendable," he said earnestly. "This is the day that our great grandparents, our forefathers, who boldly set out for the new space frontier so long ago, looked forward to with unfaltering courage. We must not fail them."

He concluded his announcement over the intercom system of the big ship by saying that the names of the crew members of the lifeboat would be given out within the hour. "And I know that every real man aboard will want to see his name there."

John Lesbee, the fifth of his line aboard, had a sinking sensation as he heard those words—and he was not mistaken.

Even as he tried to decide if he should give the signal for a desperate act of rebellion, Captain Browne made the expected announcement.

The commander said, "And I know you will all join him in his moment of pride and courage when I tell you that John Lesbee will lead the crew that carries the hopes of man in this remote area of space. And now the others—"

He thereupon named seven of the nine persons with whom Lesbee had been conspiring to seize control of the ship.

Since the lifeboat would only hold eight persons, Lesbee recognized that Browne was dispatching as many of his enemies as he could. He listened with a developing dismay, as the commander ordered all persons on the ship to come to the recreation room. "Here I request that the crew of the lifeboat join me and the other officers on stage. Their instructions are to surrender themselves to any craft which seeks to intercept them. They will be equipped with instruments whereby we here can watch, and determine the stage of scientific attainments of the dominant race on the planet below."

*

Lesbee hurried to his room on the technicians' deck, hoping that perhaps Tellier or Cantlin would seek him out there. He felt himself in need of a council of war, however brief. He waited five minutes, but not one member of his conspiratorial group showed.

Nonetheless, he had time to grow calm. Peculiarly, it was the smell of the ship that soothed him most. From the earliest days of his life, the odor of energy and the scent of metal under stress had been perpetual companions. At the moment, with the ship in orbit, there was a letting up of stress. The smell was of old energies rather than new. But the effect was similar.

He sat in the chair he used for reading, eyes closed, breathing in that complex of odors, product of so many titanic energies. Sitting there, he felt the fear leave his mind and body. He grew brave again, and strong.

Lesbee recognized soberly that his plan to seize power had involved risks. Worse, no one would question Browne's choice of him as the leader of the mission. "I am," thought Lesbee, "probably the most highly trained technician ever to be on this ship." Browne Three had taken him when he was ten, and started him on the long grind of learning that led him, one after the other, to master the mechanical skills of all the various technical departments. And Browne Four had continued his training.

He was taught how to repair relay systems. He gradually came to understand the purposes of countless analogs. The time came when he could visualize the entire automation. Long ago, the colossal cobweb of electronic instruments within the walls had become almost an extension of his nervous system.

During those years of work and study, each daily apprenticeship chore left his slim body exhausted. After he came off duty, he sought a brief relaxation and usually retired to an early rest.

He never did find the time to learn the intricate theory that underlay the ship's many operations.

His father, while he was alive, had made numerous attempts to pass his knowledge on to his son. But it was hard to teach complexities to a tired and sleepy boy. Lesbee even felt slightly relieved when his parent died. It took the pressure off him. Since then, however, he had come to realize that the Browne family, by forcing a lesser skill on the descendant of the original commander of the ship, had won their greatest victory.

As he headed finally for the recreation room, Lesbee found himself wondering: Had the Brownes trained him with the intention of preparing him for such a mission as this?

His eyes widened. If that was true, then his own conspiracy was merely an excuse. The decision to kill him might actually have been made more than a decade ago, and light years away . . . .

*

As the lifeboat fell toward Alta III, Lesbee and Tellier sat in the twin control chairs and watched on the forward screen the vast, misty atmosphere of the planet.

Tellier was thin and intellectual, a descendant of the physicist Dr. Tellier who had made many speed experiments in the early days of the voyage. It had never been understood why spaceships could not attain even a good fraction of the speed of light, let alone velocities greater than light. When the scientist met his untimely death, there was no one with the training to carry on a testing program.

It was vaguely believed by the trained personnel who succeeded Tellier that the ship had run into one of the paradoxes implicit in the Lorenz-Fitzgerald Contraction theory.

Whatever the explanation, it was never solved.

Watching Tellier, Lesbee wondered if his companion and best friend felt as empty inside as he did. Incredibly, this was the first time he—or anyone—had been outside the big ship. "We're actually heading down," he thought, "to one of those great masses of land and water, a planet."

As he watched, fascinated, the massive ball grew visibly bigger.

They came in at a slant, a long, swift, angling approach, ready to jet away if any of the natural radiation belts proved too much for their defense systems. But as each stage of radiation registered in turn, the dials showed that the lifeboat machinery made the proper responses automatically.

The silence was shattered suddenly by an alarm bell.

Simultaneously, one of the screens focused on a point of rapidly moving light far below. The light darted toward them.

A missile!

Lesbee caught his breath.

But the shining projectile veered off, turned completely around, took up position several miles away, and began to fall with them.

His first thought was: "They'll never let us land," and he experienced an intense disappointment.

Another signal brrred from the control board.

"They're probing us," said Tellier, tensely.

An instant after the words were uttered, the lifeboat seemed to shudder and to stiffen under them. It was the unmistakable feel of a tractor beam. Its field clutched the lifeboat, drew it, held it.

The science of the Alta III inhabitants was already proving itself formidable.

Underneath him the lifeboat continued its movement.

The entire crew gathered around and watched as the point of brightness resolved into an object, which rapidly grew larger. It loomed up close, bigger than they.

There was a metallic bump. The lifeboat shuddered from stem to stern.

Even before the vibrations ceased Tellier said, "Notice they put our airlock against theirs."

Behind Lesbee, his companions began that peculiar joking of the threatened. It was a coarse comedy, but it had enough actual humor suddenly to break through his fear. Involuntarily he found himself laughing.

Then, momentarily free of anxiety, aware that Browne was watching and that there was no escape, he said, "Open the airlock! Let the aliens capture us as ordered."

## II

A few minutes after the outer airlock was opened, the airlock of the alien ship folded back also. Rubberized devices rolled out and contacted the Earth lifeboat, sealing off both entrances from the vacuum of space.

Air hissed into the interlocking passageway between the two craft. In the alien craft's lock, an inner door opened.

Again Lesbee held his breath.

There was a movement in the passageway. A creature ambled into view. The being came forward with complete assurance, and pounded with something he held at the end of one of his four leathery arms on the hull.

The creature had four legs and four arms, and a long thin body held straight up. It had almost no neck, yet the many skin folds between the head and the body indicated great flexibility was possible.

Even as Lesbee noted the details of its appearance, the being turned his head slightly, and its two large expressionless eyes gazed straight at the hidden wall receptor that was photographing the scene, and therefore straight into Lesbee's eyes.

Lesbee blinked at the creature, then tore his gaze away, swallowed hard, and nodded at Tellier. "Open up!" he commanded.

The moment the inner door of the Earth lifeboat opened, six more of the four-legged beings appeared one after another in the passageway, and walked forward in the same confident way as had the first.

All seven creatures entered the open door of the lifeboat.

As they entered their thoughts came instantly into Lesbee's mind . . . .

*

As Dzing and his boarding party trotted from the small Karn ship through the connecting airlock, his chief officer thought a message to him.

"Air pressure and oxygen content are within a tiny percentage of what exists at ground level on Karn. They can certainly live on our planet."

Dzing moved forward into the Earth ship, and realized that he was in the craft's control chamber. There, for the first time, he saw the men. He and his crew ceased their forward motion; and the two groups of beings—the humans and the Karn—gazed at each other.

The appearance of the two-legged beings did not surprise Dzing. Pulse viewers had, earlier, penetrated the metal walls of the lifeboat and had accurately photographed the shape and dimension of those aboard.

His first instruction to his crew was designed to test if the strangers were, in fact, surrendering. He commanded: "Convey to the prisoners that we require them as a precaution to remove their clothing."

. . . Until that direction was given, Lesbee was still uncertain as to whether or not these beings could receive human thoughts as he was receiving theirs. From the first moment, the aliens had conducted their mental conversations *as if* they were unaware of the thoughts of the human beings. Now he watched the Karn come forward. One tugged suggestively at his clothing. And there was no doubt.

The mental telepathy was a one-way flow only—from the Karn to the humans.

He was already savoring the implications of that as he hastily undressed . . . . It was absolutely vital that Browne do not find it out.

Lesbee removed all his clothes; then, before laying them down, took out his notebook and pen. Standing there naked he wrote hurriedly:

"Don't let on that we can read the minds of these beings."

He handed the notebook around, and he felt a lot better as each of the men read it, and nodded at him silently.

Dzing communicated telepathically with someone on the ground. "These strangers," he reported, "clearly acted under command to surrender. The problem is, how can we now let them overcome us without arousing their suspicion that this is what we want them to do?"

# THE EXPENDABLES

Lesbee did not receive the answer directly. But he picked it up from Dzing's mind: "Start tearing the lifeboat apart. See if that brings a reaction."

*

The members of the Karn boarding party went to work at once. Off came the control panels; floor plates were melted and ripped up. Soon instruments, wiring, controls were exposed for examination. Most interesting of all to the aliens were the numerous computers and their accessories.

Browne must have watched the destruction; for now, before the Karn could start wrecking the automatic machinery, his voice interjected:

"Watch out, you men! I'm going to shut your airlock and cause your boat to make a sharp right turn in exactly twenty seconds."

For Lesbee and Tellier that simply meant sitting down in their chairs, and turning them so that the acceleration pressure would press them against the backs. The other men sank to the ripped-up floor, and braced themselves.

Underneath Dzing, the ship swerved. The turn began slowly, but it propelled him and his fellows over to one wall of the control room. There he grabbed with his numerous hands at some handholds that had suddenly moved out from the smooth metal. By the time the turn grew sharper, he had his four short legs braced, and he took the rest of the wide swing around with every part of his long, sleek body taut. His companions did the same.

Presently, the awful pressure eased up, and he was able to estimate that their new direction was almost at right angles to what it had been.

He had reported what was happening while it was going on. Now, the answer came: "Keep on destroying. See what they do, and be prepared to succumb to anything that looks like a lethal attack."

Lesbee wrote quickly in his notebook: "Our method of capturing them doesn't have to be subtle. They'll make it easy for us—so we can't lose."

Lesbee waited tensely as the notebook was passed around. It was still hard for him to believe that no one else had noticed what he had about this boarding party.

Tellier added a note of his own: "It's obvious now that these beings were also instructed to consider themselves expendable."

And that settled it for Lesbee. The others hadn't noticed what he had. He sighed with relief at the false analysis, for it gave him that most perfect of all advantages: that which derived from his special education.

Apparently, he alone knew enough to have analyzed what these creatures were.

The proof was in the immense clarity of their thoughts. Long ago, on earth, it had been established that man had a faltering telepathic ability, which could be utilized consistently only by electronic amplification *outside* his brain. The amount of energy needed for the step-up process was enough to burn out brain nerves, if applied directly.

Since the Karn were utilizing it directly, they couldn't be living beings.

Therefore, Dzing and his fellows were an advanced robot type.

The true inhabitants of Alta III were not risking their own skins at all.

Far more important to Lesbee, he could see how he might use these marvellous mechanisms to defeat Browne, take over the *Hope of Man*, and start the long journey back to Earth.

### III

He had been watching the Karn at their work of destruction, while he had these thoughts. Now, he said aloud: "Hainker, Graves."

"Yes?" The two men spoke together.

"In a few moments I'm going to ask Captain Browne to turn the ship again. When he does, use our specimen gas guns!"

The men grinned with relief. "Consider it done," said Hainker.

Lesbee ordered the other four crewmen to be ready to use the specimen-holding devices at top speed. To Tellier he said, "You take charge if anything happens to me."

Then he wrote one more message in the notebook: "These beings will probably continue their mental intercommunication after they are apparently rendered unconscious. Pay no attention, and do not comment on it in any way."

He felt a lot better when that statement also had been read by the others, and the notebook was once more in his possession. Quickly, he spoke to the screen:

"Captain Browne! Make another turn, just enough to pin them."

And so they captured Dzing and his crew.

As he had expected, the Karn continued their telepathic conversation. Dzing reported to his ground contact: "I think we did that rather well."

There must have been an answering message from below, because he went on, "Yes, commander. We are now prisoners as per your instructions, and shall await events . . . . The imprisoning method? Each of us is pinned down by a machine which has been placed astride us, with the main section adjusted to the contour of our bodies. A series of rigid metal appendages fasten our arms and legs. All these devices are electronically controlled, and we can of course escape at any time. Naturally, such action is for later . . . ."

Lesbee was chilled by the analysis; but for expendables there was no turning back.

He ordered his men: "Get dressed. Then start repairing the ship. Put all the floor plates back except the section at G-8. They removed some of the analogs, and I'd better make sure myself that it all goes back all right."

When he had dressed, he re-set the course of the lifeboat, and called Browne. The screen lit up after a moment, and there staring back at him was the unhappy countenance of the forty-year-old officer.

Browne said glumly: "I want to congratulate you and your crew on your accomplishments. It would seem that we have a small scientific superiority over this race, and that we can attempt a limited landing."

Since there would never be a landing on Alta III, Lesbee simply waited without comment as Browne seemed lost in thought.

The officer stirred finally. He still seemed uncertain. "Mr. Lesbee," he said, "as you must understand, this is an extremely dangerous situation for me—and—" he added hastily—"for this entire expedition."

What struck Lesbee, as he heard those words, was that Browne was not going to let him back on the ship. But he had to get aboard to accomplish his own purpose. He thought: "I'll have to bring this whole conspiracy out into the open, and apparently make a compromise offer."

He drew a deep breath, gazed straight into the eyes of Browne's image on the screen and said with the complete courage of a man for whom there is no turning back: "It seems to me, sir, that we have two alternatives. We can resolve all these personal problems either through a democratic election or by a joint captaincy, you being one of the captains and I being the other."

*

To any other person who might have been listening the remark must have seemed a complete non sequitur. Browne, however, understood its relevance. He said with a sneer, "So you're out in the open. Well, let me tell you, Mr. Lesbee, there was never any talk of elections when the Lesbees were in power. And for a very good reason. A spaceship requires a technical aristocracy to command it. As for a joint captaincy, it wouldn't work."

Lesbee urged his lie: "If we're going to stay here, we'll need at least two people of equal authority—one on the ground, one on the ship."

"I couldn't trust you on the ship!" said Browne flatly.

"Then you be on the ship," Lesbee proposed. "All such practical details can be arranged."

The older man must have been almost beside himself with the intensity of his own feelings on this subject. He flashed, "Your family has been out of power for over fifty years! How can you still feel that you have any rights?"

Lesbee countered, "How come you still know what I'm talking about?"

Browne said, a grinding rage in his tone, "The concept of inherited power was introduced by the first Lesbee. It was never planned."

"But here you are," said Lesbee, "yourself a beneficiary of inherited power."

Browne said from between clenched teeth: "It's absolutely ridiculous that the Earth government which was in power when the ship left—and every member of which has been long dead—should appoint somebody to a command position . . . and that now his descendant think that command post should be his, and his family's, for all time!"

Lesbee was silent, startled by the dark emotions he had uncovered in the man. He felt even more justified, if that were possible, and advanced his next suggestion without a qualm.

"Captain, this is a crisis. We should postpone our private struggle. Why don't we bring one of these prisoners aboard so that we can question him by use of films, or play acting? Later, we can discuss your situation and mine."

He saw from the look on Browne's face that the reasonableness of the suggestion, *and its potentialities*, were penetrating.

Browne said quickly, "Only you come aboard—and with one prisoner only. No one else!"

Lesbee felt a dizzying thrill as the man responded to his bait. He thought: "It's like an exercise in logic. He'll try to murder me as soon as he gets me alone and is satisfied that he can attack without danger to himself. But that very scheme is what will get me aboard. And I've got to get on the ship to carry out *my* plan."

Browne was frowning. He said in a concerned tone: "Mr. Lesbee, can you think of any reason why we should not bring one of these beings aboard?"

Lesbee shook his head. "No reason, sir," he lied.

Browne seemed to come to a decision. "Very well. I'll see you shortly, and we can then discuss additional details."

Lesbee dared not say another word. He nodded, and broke the connection, shuddering, disturbed, uneasy.

"But," he thought, "what else can we do?"

*

He turned his attention to the part of the floor that had been left open for him. Quickly, he bent down and studied the codes on each of the programming units, as if he were seeking exactly the right ones that had originally been in those slots.

He found the series he wanted: an intricate system of cross-connected units that had originally been designed to program a remote-control landing system, an advanced Waldo mechanism capable of landing the craft on a planet and taking off again, all directed on the pulse level of human thought.

He slid each unit of the series into its sequential position and locked it in.

Then, that important task completed, he picked up the remote control attachment for the series and casually put it in his pocket.

He returned to the control board and spent several minutes examining the wiring and comparing it with a wall chart. A number of wires had been torn loose. These he now re-connected, and at the same time he managed with a twist of his pliers to short-circuit a key relay of the remote control pilot.

Lesbee replaced the panel itself loosely. There was no time to connect it properly. And, since he could easily justify his next move, he pulled a cage out of the store-room. Into this he hoisted Dzing, manacles and all.

Before lowering the lid he rigged into the cage a simple resistor that would prevent the Karn from broadcasting on the human thought level. The device was simple merely in that it was not selective. It had an on-off switch which triggered, or stopped, energy flow in the metal walls on the thought level.

When the device was installed, Lesbee slipped the tiny remote control for *it* into his other pocket. He did not activate the control. Not yet.

From the cage Dzing telepathed: "It is significant that these beings have selected me for this special attention. We might conclude that it is a matter of mathematical accident, or else that they are very observant and so noticed that I was the one who directed activities. Whatever the reason, it would be foolish to turn back now."

A bell began to ring. As Lesbee watched, a spot of light appeared high on one of the screens. It moved rapidly toward some crossed lines in the exact center of the screen. Inexorably, then, the *Hope of Man*, as represented by the light, and the lifeboat moved toward their fateful rendezvous.

IV

Browne's instructions were: "Come to Control Room Below!"

Lesbee guided his powered dolly with the cage on it out of the big ship's airlock—and saw that the man in the control room of the lock was Second Officer Selwyn. Heavy brass for such a routine task. Selwyn waved at him with a twisted smile as Lesbee wheeled his cargo along the silent corridor.

He saw no one else on his route. Other personnel had evidently been cleared from this part of the vessel. A little later, grim and determined, he set the cage down in the center of the big room and anchored it magnetically to the floor.

As Lesbee entered the captain's office, Browne looked up from one of the two control chairs and stepped down from the rubber-sheathed dais to the same level as Lesbee. He came forward, smiling, and held out his hand. He was a big man, as all the Brownes had been, bigger by a head than Lesbee, good-looking in a clean-cut way. The two men were alone.

"I'm glad you were so frank," he said. "I doubt if I could have spoken so bluntly to you without your initiative as an example."

But as they shook hands, Lesbee was wary and suspicious. Lesbee thought: "He's trying to recover from the insanity of his reaction. I really blew him wide open."

Browne continued in the same hearty tone: "I've made up my mind. An election is out of the question. The ship is swarming with untrained dissident groups, most of which simply want to go back to Earth."

Lesbee, who had the same desire, was discreetly silent.

Browne said, "You'll be ground captain; I'll be ship captain. Why don't we sit down right now and work out a communique on which we can agree and that I can read over the intercom to the others?"

As Lesbee seated himself in the chair beside Browne, he was thinking: "What can be gained from publicly naming me ground captain?"

He concluded finally, cynically, that the older man could gain the confidence of John Lesbee—lull him, lead him on, delude him, destroy him.

Surreptitiously Lesbee examined the room. Control Room Below was a large square chamber adjoining the massive central engines. Its control board was a duplicate of the one on the bridge located at the top of the ship. The great vessel could be guided equally from either board, except that pre-emptive power was on the bridge. The officer of the watch was given the right to make Merit decisions in an emergency.

Lesbee made a quick mental calculation, and deduced that it was First Officer Miller's watch on the bridge. Miller was a staunch supporter of Browne. The man was probably watching them on one of his screens, ready to come to Browne's aid at a moment's notice.

*

A few minutes later, Lesbee listened thoughtfully as Browne read their joint communique over the intercom, designating him as ground captain. He found himself a little amazed, and considerably dismayed, at the absolute confidence the older man must feel about his own power and position on the ship. It was a big step, naming his chief rival to so high a rank.

Browne's next act was equally surprising. While they were still on the viewers, Browne reached over, clapped Lesbee affectionately on the shoulders and said to the watching audience:

"As you all know, John is the only direct descendant of the original captain. No one knows exactly what happened half a hundred years ago when my grandfather first took command. But I remember the old man always felt that only he understood how things should be. I doubt if he had any confidence in *any* young whippersnapper over whom he did not have complete control. I often felt that my father was the victim rather than the beneficiary of my grandfather's temper and feelings of superiority."

Browne smiled engagingly. "Anyway, good people, though we can't unbreak the eggs that were broken then, we can certainly start healing the wounds, without—" his tone was suddenly firm—"negating the fact that my own training and experience make me the proper commander of the ship itself."

He broke off. "Captain Lesbee and I shall now jointly attempt to communicate with the captured intelligent life form from the planet below. You may watch, though we reserve the right to cut you off for good reason." He turned to Lesbee. "What do you think we should do first, John?"

Lesbee was in a dilemma. The first large doubt had come to him, the possibility that perhaps the other was sincere. The possibility was especially disturbing because in a few moments a part of his own plan would be revealed.

He sighed, and realized that there was no turning back at this stage. He thought: "We'll have to bring the entire madness out into the open, and only then can we begin to consider agreement as real."

Aloud, he said in a steady voice, "Why not bring the prisoner out where we can see him?"

As the tractor beam lifted Dzing out of the cage, and thus away from the energies that had suppressed his thought waves, the Karn telepathed to his contact on Alta III:

"Have been held in a confined space, the metal of which was energized against communication. I shall now attempt to perceive and evaluate the condition and performance of this ship—"

At that point, Browne reached over and clicked off the intercom. Having shut off the audience, he turned accusingly to Lesbee, and said, "Explain your failure to inform me that these beings communicated by telepathy."

The tone of his voice was threatening. There was a hint of angry color in his face. It was the moment of discovery.

*

Lesbee hesitated, and then simply pointed out how precarious their relationship had been. He finished frankly, "I thought by keeping it a secret I might be able to stay alive a little longer, which was certainly not what you intended when you sent me out as an expendable."

Browne snapped, "But how did you hope to utilize?—"

He stopped. "Never mind," he muttered.

Dzing was telepathing again:

"In many ways this is mechanically a very advanced type ship. Atomic energy drives are correctly installed. The automatic machinery performs magnificently. There is massive energy screen equipment, and they can put out a tractor beam to match anything we have that's mobile. But there is a wrongness in the energy flows of this ship, which I lack the experience to interpret. Let me furnish you some data . . . ."

The data consisted of variable wave measurements, evidently—so Lesbee deduced—the wave-lengths of the energy flows involved in the "wrongness."

He said in alarm at that point, "Better drop him into the cage while we analyze what he could be talking about."

Browne did so—as Dzing telepathed: "If what you suggest is true, then these beings are completely at our mercy—"

Cut off!

Browne was turning on the intercom. "Sorry I had to cut you good people off," he said. "You'll be interested to know that we have managed to tune in on the thought pulses of the prisoner and have intercepted his calls to someone on the planet below. This gives us an advantage." He turned to Lesbee. "Don't you agree?"

Browne visibly showed no anxiety, whereas Dzing's final statement flabbergasted Lesbee. " . . . *completely at our mercy* . . . " surely meant exactly that. He was staggered that Browne could have missed the momentous meaning.

Browne addressed him enthusiastically, "I'm excited by this telepathy! It's a marvelous short-cut to communication, if we could build up our own thought pulses. Maybe we could use the principle of the remote-control landing device which, as you know, can project human thoughts on a simple, gross level, where ordinary energies get confused by the intense field needed for the landing."

What interested Lesbee in the suggestion was that he had in his pocket a remote control for precisely such mechanically produced thought pulses. Unfortunately, the control was for the lifeboat. It probably would be advisable to tune the control to the ship landing system also. It was a problem he had thought of earlier, and now Browne had opened the way for an easy solution.

He held his voice steady as he said, "Captain, let me program those landing analogs while you prepare the film communication project. That way we can be ready for him either way."

Browne seemed to be completely trusting, for he agreed at once.

At Browne's direction, a film projector was wheeled in. It was swiftly mounted on solid connections at one end of the room. The cameraman and Third Officer Mindel—who had come in with him—strapped themselves into two adjoining chairs attached to the projector, and were evidently ready.

*

While this was going on, Lesbee called various technical personnel. Only one technician protested. "But, John," he said, "that way we have a double control—with the lifeboat control having pre-emption over the ship. That's very unusual."

It was unusual. But it was the lifeboat control that was in his pocket where he could reach it quickly; and so he said adamantly, "Do you want to talk to Captain Browne? Do you want his okay?"

"No, no." The technician's doubts seemed to subside. "I heard you being named joint captain. You're the boss. It shall be done."

Lesbee put down the closed-circuit phone into which he had been talking, and turned. It was then he saw that the film was ready to roll, and that Browne had his fingers on the controls of the tractor beam. The older man stared at him questioningly.

"Shall I go ahead?" he asked.

At this penultimate moment, Lesbee had a qualm.

Almost immediately he realized that the only alternative to what Browne planned was that he reveal his own secret knowledge.

He hesitated, torn by doubts. Then: "Will you turn that off?" He indicated the intercom.

Browne said to the audience, "We'll bring you in again on this in a minute, good people." He broke the connection and gazed questioningly at Lesbee.

Whereupon Lesbee said in a low voice, "Captain, I should inform you that I brought the Karn aboard in the hope of using him against you."

"Well, that is a frank and open admission," the officer replied very softly.

"I mention this," said Lesbee, "because if you had similar ulterior motives, we should clear the air completely before proceeding with this attempt at communication."

A blossom of color spread from Browne's neck over his face. At last he said slowly, "I don't know how I can convince you, but I had no schemes."

Lesbee gazed at Browne's open countenance, and suddenly he realized that the officer was sincere. Browne had accepted the compromise. The solution of a joint captaincy was agreeable to him.

Sitting there, Lesbee experienced an enormous joy. Seconds went by before he realized what underlay the intense pleasurable excitement. It was simply the discovery that—communication worked. You could tell your truth and get a hearing . . . if it made sense.

It seemed to him that his truth made a lot of sense. He was offering Browne peace aboard the ship. Peace at a price, of course; but still peace. And in this severe emergency Browne recognized the entire validity of the solution.

So it was now evident to Lesbee.

Without further hesitation he told Browne that the creatures who had boarded the lifeboat, were robots—not alive at all.

\*

Browne was nodding thoughtfully. Finally he said: "But I don't see how this could be utilized to take over the ship."

Lesbee said patiently, "As you know, sir, the remote landing control system includes five principal ideas which are projected very forcibly on the thought level.

# The Expendables

Three of these are for guidance—up, down and sideways. Intense magnetic fields, any one of which could partially jam a complex robot's thinking processes. The fourth and fifth are instructions to blast either up or down. The force of the blast depends on how far the control is turned on. Since the energy used is overwhelming those simple commands would take pre-emption over the robot. When that first one came aboard the lifeboat, I had a scan receiver—nondetectable—on him. This registered two power sources, one pointing forward, one backward, from the chest level. That's why I had him on his back when I brought him in here. But the fact is I could have had him tilted and pointing at a target, and activated either control four or five, thus destroying whatever was in the path of the resulting blast. Naturally, I took all possible precautions to make sure that this did not happen until you had indicated what you intended to do. One of these precautions would enable us to catch this creature's thoughts without—"

As he was speaking, he eagerly put his hand into his pocket, intending to show the older man the tiny on-off control device by which—when it was off—they would be able to read Dzing's thoughts without removing him from the cage.

He stopped short in his explanation, because an ugly expression had come suddenly into Browne's face.

The big man glanced at Third Officer Mindel. "Well, Dan," he said, "do you think that's it?"

Lesbee noticed with shock that Mindel had on sound amplifying earphones. He must have overheard every word that Browne and he had spoken to each other.

Mindel nodded. "Yes, Captain," he said. "I very definitely think he has now told us what we wanted to find out."

Lesbee grew aware that Browne had released himself from his acceleration safety belt and was stepping away from his seat. The officer turned and, standing very straight, said in a formal tone:

"Technician Lesbee, we have heard your admission of gross dereliction of duty, conspiracy to overthrow the lawful government of this ship, scheme to utilize alien creatures to destroy human beings, and confession of other unspeakable crimes. In this extremely dangerous situation, summary execution without formal trial is justified. I therefore sentence you to death and order Third Officer Dan Mindel to—"

He faltered, and came to a stop.

## V

Two things had been happening as he talked, Lesbee squeezed the "off" switch of the cage control, an entirely automatic gesture, convulsive, a spasmodic movement, result of his dismay. It was a mindless gesture. So far as he knew consciously, freeing Dzing's thoughts had no useful possibility for him. His only real hope—as he realized almost immediately—was to get his other hand into his remaining coat pocket and with it manipulate the remote-control landing device, the secret of which he had so naively revealed to Browne.

The second thing that happened was that Dzing, released from mental control, telepathed:

"Free again—and this time of course permanently! I have just now activated by remote control the relays that will in a few moments start the engines of this ship, and I have naturally re-set the mechanism for controlling the rate of acceleration—"

His thoughts must have impinged progressively on Browne, for it was at that point that the officer paused uncertainly.

Dzing continued: "I verified your analysis. This vessel does not have the internal energy flows of an interstellar ship. These two-legged beings have therefore failed to achieve the Light Speed Effect which alone makes possible trans-light velocities. I suspect they have taken many generations to make this journey, are far indeed for their home base, and I'm sure I can capture them all."

Lesbee reached over, tripped on the intercom and yelled at the screen: "All stations prepare for emergency acceleration! Grab anything!"

To Browne he shouted: "Get to your seat—*quick!*"

His actions were automatic responses to danger. Only after the words were spoken did it occur to him that he had no interest in the survival of Captain Browne. And that in fact the only reason the man was in danger was because he had stepped away from his safety belt, so that Mindel's blaster would kill Lesbee without damaging Browne.

Browne evidently understood his danger. He started toward the control chair from which he had released himself only moments before. His reaching hands were still a foot or more from it when the impact of Acceleration One stopped him. He stood there trembling like a man who had struck an invisible but palpable wall. The next instant Acceleration Two caught him and thrust him on his back to the floor. He began to slide toward the rear of the room, faster and faster, and because he was quick and understanding he pressed the palms of his hands and his rubber shoes hard against the floor and so tried to slow the movement of his body.

Lesbee was picturing other people elsewhere in the ship desperately trying to save themselves. He groaned, for the commander's failure was probably being duplicated everywhere.

Even as he had that thought, Acceleration Three caught Browne. Like a rock propelled by a catapult he shot toward the rear wall. It was cushioned to protect human beings, and so it reacted like rubber, bouncing him a little. But the stuff had only momentary resilience.

Acceleration Four pinned Browne halfway into the cushioned wall. From its imprisoning depths, he managed a strangled yell.

"Lesbee, put a tractor beam on me! Save me! I'll make it up to you. I—"

Acceleration Five choked off the words.

The man's appeal brought momentary wonder to Lesbee. He was amazed that Browne hoped for mercy . . . after what had happened.

Browne's anguished words did produce one effect in him. They reminded him that there was something he must do. He forced his hand and his arm to the control board and focussed a tractor beam that firmly captured Third Officer Mindel and the cameraman. His intense effort was barely in time. Acceleration followed acceleration, making movement impossible. The time between each surge of increased speed grew longer. The slow minutes lengthened into what seemed an hour, then many hours. Lesbee was held in his chair as if he were gripped by hands of steel. His eyes felt glassy; his body had long since lost all feeling.

He noticed something.

The rate of acceleration was different from what the original Tellier had prescribed long ago. The actual increase in forward pressure each time was less.

He realized something else. For a long time, no thoughts had come from the Karn.

*

Suddenly, he felt an odd shift in speed. A physical sensation of slight, very slight, angular movement accompanied the maneuver.

Slowly, the metal-like bands let go of his body. The numb feeling was replaced by the pricking as of thousands of tiny needles. Instead of muscle-compressing acceleration there was only a steady pressure.

It was the pressure that he had in the past equated with gravity.

Lesbee stirred hopefully, and when he felt himself move, realized what had happened. The artificial gravity had been shut off. Simultaneously, the ship had made a half turn within its outer shell. The drive power was now coming from below, a constant one gravity thrust.

At this late, late moment, he plunged his hand into the pocket which held the remote control for the pilotless landing mechanism—and activated it.

"That ought to turn on his thoughts," he told himself savagely.

But if Dzing was telepathing to his masters, it was no longer on the human thought level. So Lesbee concluded unhappily.

The ether was silent.

He now grew aware of something more. The ship smelled different: better, cleaner, purer.

Lesbee's gaze snapped over to the speed dials on the control board. The figures registering there were unbelievable. They indicated that the spaceship was traveling at a solid fraction of the speed of light.

Lesbee stared at the numbers incredulously. "We didn't have time!" he thought. "How could we go so fast so quickly—in hours only to near the speed of light!"

Sitting there, breathing hard, fighting to recover from the effects of that prolonged speed-up, he felt the fantastic reality of the universe. During all this slow century of flight through space, the *Hope of Man* had had the potential for this vastly greater velocity.

He visualized the acceleration series so expertly programmed by Dzing as having achieved a shift to a new state of matter in motion. The "light speed effect," the Karn robot had called it.

"And Tellier missed it," he thought.

All those experiments the physicist had performed so painstakingly, and left a record of, had missed the great discovery.

Missed it! And so a shipload of human beings had wandered for generations through the black deeps of interstellar space.

\*

Across the room Browne was climbing groggily to his feet. He muttered, " . . . Better get back to . . . control chair."

He had taken only a few uncertain steps when a realization seemed to strike him. He looked up then, and stared wildly at Lesbee. "Oh!" he said. The sound came from the gut level, a gasp of horrified understanding.

As he slapped a complex of tractor beams on Browne, Lesbee said, "That's right, you're looking at your enemy. Better start talking. We haven't much time."

Browne was pale now. But his mouth had been left free and so he was able to say huskily, "I did what any lawful government does in an emergency. I dealt with treason summarily, taking time only to find out what it consisted of."

Lesbee had had another thought, this time about Miller on the bridge. Hastily, he swung Browne over in front of him. "Hand me your blaster," he said. "Stock first."

He freed the other's arm, so that he could reach into the holster and take it out.

Lesbee felt a lot better when he had the weapon. But still another idea had come to him. He said harshly, "I want to lift you over to the cage, and I don't want First Officer Miller to interfere. Get that, *Mister* Miller!"

There was no answer from the screen.

Browne said uneasily, "Why over to the cage?"

Lesbee did not answer right away. Silently he manipulated the tractor beam control until Browne was in position. Having gotten him there, Lesbee hesitated. What bothered him was, why had the Karn's thought impulses ceased? He had an awful feeling that something was very wrong indeed.

He gulped, and said, "Raise the lid!"

Again, he freed Browne's arm. The big man reached over gingerly, unfastened the catch, and then drew back and glanced questioningly at Lesbee.

"Look inside!" Lesbee commanded.

Browne said scathingly, "You don't think for one second that—" He stopped, for he was peering into the cage. He uttered a cry: "He's gone!"

## VI

Lesbee discussed the disappearance with Browne.

It was an abrupt decision on his part to do so. The question of where Dzing might have got to was not something he should merely turn over in his own head.

He began by pointing at the dials from which the immense speed of the ship could be computed, and then, when that meaning was absorbed by the older man, said simply, "What happened? Where did he go? And how could we speed up to just under 186,000 miles a second in so short a time?"

He had lowered the big man to the floor, and now he took some of the tension from the tractor beam but did not release the power. Browne stood in apparent deep thought. Finally, he nodded. "All right," he said, "I know what happened."

"Tell me."

Browne changed the subject, said in a deliberate tone, "What are you going to do with me?"

Lesbee stared at him for a moment unbelievingly. "You're going to withhold this information?" he demanded.

Browne spread his hands. "What else can I do? Till I know my fate, I have nothing to lose."

Lesbee suppressed a strong impulse to rush over and strike his prisoner. He said finally, "In your judgment is this delay dangerous?"

Browne was silent, but a bead of sweat trickled down his cheek. "I have nothing to lose," he repeated.

The expression in Lesbee's face must have alarmed him, for he went on quickly, "Look, there's no need for you to conspire any more. What you really want is to go home, isn't it? Don't you see, with this new method of acceleration, we can make it to Earth in a few *months!*"

He stopped. He seemed momentarily uncertain.

Lesbee snapped angrily, "Who are you trying to fool? Months! We're a dozen light years in actual distance from Earth. You mean years, not months."

Browne hesitated then: "All right, a few years. But at least not a lifetime. So if you'll promise not to scheme against me further, I'll promise—"

"*You'll* promise!" Lesbee spoke savagely. He had been taken aback by Browne's instant attempt at blackmail. But the momentary sense of defeat was gone. He knew with a stubborn rage that he would stand for no nonsense.

He said in an uncompromising voice, "Mister Browne, twenty seconds after I stop speaking, you start talking. If you don't, I'll batter you against these walls. I mean it!"

Browne was pale. "Are you going to kill me? That's all I want to know. Look—" his tone was urgent—"we don't have to fight any more. We can go home. Don't you see? The long madness is just about over. Nobody has to die."

Lesbee hesitated. What the big man said was at least partly true. There was an attempt here to make twelve years sound like twelve days, or at most twelve weeks. But the fact was, it *was* a short period compared to the century-long journey which, at one time, had been the only possibility.

\*

He thought: "Am I going to kill him?"

# THE EXPENDABLES

It was hard to believe that he would, under the circumstances. All right. If not death, then what? He sat there uncertain. The vital seconds went by, and he could see no solution. He thought finally, in desperation: "I'll have to give in for the moment. Even a minute thinking about this is absolutely crazy."

He said aloud in utter frustration, "I'll promise you this. If you can figure out how I can feel safe in a ship commanded by you I'll give your plan consideration. And now, mister, start talking."

Browne nodded. "I accept that promise," he said. "What we've run into here is the Lorenz-Fitzgerald Contraction Theory. Only it's not a theory any more. We're living the reality of it."

Lesbee argued, "But it only took us a few hours to get to the speed of light."

Browne said, "As we approach light speed, space foreshortens and time compresses. What seemed like a few hours would be days in normal time and space."

What Browne explained then was different rather than difficult. Lesbee had to blink his mind to shut out the glare of his old ideas and habits of thought, so that the more subtle shades of super-speed phenomena could shine through into his awareness.

The time compression—as Browne explained it—was gradational. The rapid initial series of accelerations were obviously designed to pin down the personnel of the ship. Subsequent increments would be according to what was necessary to attain the ultra-speed finally achieved.

Since the drive was still on, it was clear that some resistance was being encountered, perhaps from the fabric of space itself.

It was no time to discuss technical details. Lesbee accepted the remarkable reality and said quickly, "Yes, but where is Dzing?"

"My guess," said Browne, "is that he did not come along."

"How do you mean?"

"The space-time foreshortening did not affect him."

"But—" Lesbee began blankly.

"Look," said Browne harshly, "don't ask me how he did it. My picture is, he stayed in the cage till after the acceleration stopped. Then, in a leisurely fashion, he released himself from the electrically locked manacles, climbed out, and went off to some other part of the ship. He wouldn't have to hurry since by this time he was operating at a rate of, say, five hundred times faster than our living pace."

26

Lesbee said, "But that means he's been out there for hours—his time. What's he been up to?"

Browne admitted that he had no answer for that.

"But you can see," he pointed out anxiously, "that I meant what I said about going back to Earth. We have no business in this part of space. These beings are far ahead of us scientifically."

His purpose was obviously to persuade. Lesbee thought: "He's back to *our* fight. That's more important to him than any damage the real enemy is causing."

A vague recollection came of the things he had read about the struggle for power throughout Earth history. How men intrigued for supremacy while vast hordes of the invader battered down the gates. Browne was a true spiritual descendant of all those mad people.

Slowly, Lesbee turned and faced the big board. What was baffling to him was, what could you do against a being who moved five hundred times as fast as you did?

## VII

He had a sudden sense of awe, a picture . . . . At any given instant Dzing was a blur. A spot of light. A movement so rapid that, even as the gaze lighted on him, he was gone to the other end of the ship—and back.

Yet Lesbee knew it took time to traverse the great ship from end to end. Twenty, even twenty-five minutes, was normal walking time for a human being going along the corridor known as Center A.

It would take the Karn a full six seconds there and back. In its way that was a significant span of time, but after Lesbee had considered it for a moment he felt appalled.

What could they do against a creature who had so great a time differential in his favor?

From behind him, Browne said, "Why don't you use against him that remote landing control system that you set up with my permission?"

Lesbee confessed: "I did that, as soon as the acceleration ceased. But he must have been—back—in the faster time by then."

"That wouldn't make any difference," said Browne.

"Eh!" Lesbee was startled.

Browne parted his lips evidently intending to explain, and then he closed them again. Finally he said, "Make sure the intercom is off."

Lesbee did so. But he was realizing that Browne was up to something again. He said, and there was rage in his tone, "I don't get it, and you do. Is that right."

"Yes," said Browne. He spoke deliberately, but he was visibly suppressing excitement. "I know how to defeat this creature. That puts me in a bargaining position."

Lesbee's eyes were narrowed to slits. "Damn you, no bargain. Tell me, or else!"

Browne said, "I'm not really trying to be difficult. You either have to kill me, or come to some agreement. I want to know what that agreement is, because of course I'll do it."

Lesbee said, "I think we ought to have an election."

"I agree!" Browne spoke instantly. "You set it up." He broke off. "And now release me from these tractors and I'll show you the neatest space-time trick you've ever seen, and that'll be the end of Dzing."

Lesbee gazed at the man's face, saw there the same openness of countenance, the same frank honest that had preceded the execution order, and he thought, "What can he do?"

He considered many possibilities, and thought finally, desperately: "He's got the advantage over me of superior knowledge—the most undefeatable weapon in the world. The only thing I can really hope to use against it in the final issue is *my* knowledge of a multitude of technician-level details."

But—what could Browne do against Lesbee?

He said unhappily to the other, "Before I free you, I want to lift you over to Mindel. When I do, you get his blaster for me."

"Sure," said Browne casually.

A few moments later he handed Mindel's gun over to Lesbee. So that wasn't it.

Lesbee thought: "There's Miller on the bridge—can it be that Miller flashed him a ready signal when my back was turned to the board?"

Perhaps, like Browne, Miller had been temporarily incapacitated during the period of acceleration. It was vital that he find out Miller's present capability.

*

Lesbee tripped the intercom between the two boards. The rugged, lined face of the first officer showed large on the screen. Lesbee could see the outlines of the bridge behind the man and, beyond, the starry blackness of space. Lesbee said courteously, "Mr. Miller, how did you make out during the acceleration?"

"It caught me by surprise, Captain. I really got a battering. I think I was out for

28

a while. But I'm all right now."

"Good," said Lesbee. "As you probably heard, Captain Browne and I have come to an agreement, and we are now going to destroy the creature that is loose on the ship. Stand by!"

Cynically, he broke the connection.

Miller was there all right, waiting. But the question was still, what could Miller do? The answer of course was that Miller could pre-empt. And—Lesbee asked himself—what could *that* do?

Abruptly, it seemed to him, he had the answer.

It was the technician's answer that he had been mentally straining for.

He now understood Browne's plan. They were waiting for Lesbee to let down his guard for a moment. Then Miller would pre-empt, cut off the tractor beam from Browne and seize Lesbee with it.

For the two officers it was vital that Lesbee not have time to fire the blaster at Browne. Lesbee thought: "It's the only thing they can be worried about. The truth is, there's nothing else to stop them."

The solution was, Lesbee realized with a savage glee, to let the two men achieve their desire. But first—

"Mr. Browne," he said quietly, "I think you should give your information. If I agree that it is indeed the correct solution, I shall release you and we shall have an election. You and I will stay right here till the election is over."

Browne said, "I accept your promise. The speed of light is a constant, and does not change in relation to moving objects. That would also apply to electromagnetic fields."

Lesbee said, "Then Dzing was affected by the remote-control device I turned on."

"Instantly," said Browne. "He never got a chance to do anything. How much power did you use?"

"Only first stage," said Lesbee. "But the machine-driven thought pulses in that would interfere with just about every magnetic field in his body. He couldn't do another coherent thing."

Browne said in a hushed tone, "It's got to be. He'll be out of control in one of the corridors, completely at our mercy." He grinned. "I told you I knew how to defeat him—because, of course, he was already defeated."

Lesbee considered that for a long moment, eyes narrowed. He realized that he accepted the explanation, but that he had preparations to make, and quickly—before

Browne got suspicious of his delay.

He turned to the board and switched on the intercom. "People," he said, "strap yourselves in again. Help those who were injured to do the same. We may have another emergency. You have several minutes, I think, but don't waste any of them."

He cut off the intercom, and he activated the closed-circuit intercom of the technical stations. He said urgently, "Special instruction to Technical personnel. Report anything unusual, particularly if strange thought forms are going through your mind."

He had an answer to that within moments after he finished speaking. A man's twangy voice came over: "I keep thinking I'm somebody named Dzing, and I'm trying to report to my owners. Boy, am I incoherent!"

"Where is this?"

"D—4—19."

Lesbee punched the buttons that gave them a TV view of that particular ship location. Almost immediately he spotted a shimmer near the floor.

After a moment's survey he ordered a heavy-duty mobile blaster brought to the corridor. By the time its colossal energies ceased, Dzing was only a darkened area on the flat surface.

*

While these events were progressing, Lesbee had kept one eye on Browne and Mindel's blaster firmly gripped in his left hand. Now he said, "Well, sir, you certainly did what you promised. Wait a moment while I put this gun away, and then I'll carry out my part of the bargain."

He started to do so, then, out of pity, paused.

He had been thinking in the back of his mind about what Browne had said earlier: that the trip to Earth might only take a few months. The officer had backed away from that statement, but it had been bothering Lesbee ever since.

If it were true, then it was indeed a fact that nobody need die!

He said quickly, "What was your reason for saying that the journey home would only take—well—less than a year?"

"It's the tremendous time compression," Browne explained eagerly. "The distance as you pointed out is over 12 light-years. But with a time ratio of 3, 4, or 500 to one, we'll make it in less than a month. When I first started to say that, I could see that the figures were incomprehensible to you in your tense mood. In fact, I could scarcely believe them myself."

Lesbee said, staggered, "We can get back to Earth in a couple of weeks—my God!" He broke off, said urgently, "Look, I accept you as commander. We don't need an election. The status quo is good enough for any short period of time. Do you agree?"

"Of course," said Browne. "That's the point I've been trying to make."

As he spoke, his face was utterly guileless.

Lesbee gazed at that mask of innocence, and he thought hopelessly: "What's wrong? Why isn't he really agreeing? Is it because he doesn't want to lose his command so quickly?"

Sitting there, unhappily fighting for the other's life, he tried to place himself mentally in the position of the commander of a vessel, tried to look at the prospect of a return to view. It was hard to picture such a reality. But presently it seemed to him that he understood.

He said gently, feeling his way, "It would be kind of a shame to return without having made a successful landing anywhere. With this new speed, we could visit a dozen sun systems, and still get home in a year."

The look that came into Browne's face for a fleeting moment told Lesbee that he had penetrated to the thought in the man's mind.

The next instant, Browne was shaking his head vigorously. "This is no time for side excursions," he said. "We'll leave explorations of new star systems to future expeditions. The people of this ship have served their term. We go straight home."

Browne's face was now completely relaxed. His blue eyes shone with truth and sincerity.

There was nothing further that Lesbee could say. The gulf between Browne and himself could not be bridged.

The commander had to kill his rival, so that he might finally return to Earth and report that the mission of the *Hope of Man* was accomplished.

## VIII

In the most deliberate fashion Lesbee shoved the blaster into the inner pocket of his coat. Then, as if he were being careful, he used the tractor beam to push Browne about four feet away. There he set him down, released him from the beam, and—with the same deliberateness—drew his hand away from the tractor controls. Thus he made himself completely defenseless.

# THE EXPENDABLES

It was the moment of vulnerability.

Browne leaped at him, yelling: "Miller—pre-empt!"

First Officer Miller obeyed the command of his captain.

What happened then, only Lesbee, the technician with a thousand bits of detailed knowledge, expected.

For years it had been observed that when Control Room Below took over from Bridge, the ship speeded up slightly. And when Bridge took over from Control Room Below, the ship slowed instantly by the same amount—in each instance, something less than half a mile an hour.

The two boards were not completely synchronized. The technicians often joked about it, and Lesbee had once read an obscure technical explanation for the discrepancy. It had to do with the impossibility of ever getting two metals refined to the same precision of internal structure.

It was the age-old story of no two objects in the universe are alike. But in times past, the differential had meant nothing. It was a technical curiosity, an interesting phenomenon of the science of metallurgy, a practical problem that caused machinists to curse good-naturedly when technicians like Lesbee required them to make a replacement part.

Unfortunately for Browne, the ship was now traveling near the speed of light.

His strong hands, reaching towards Lesbee's slighter body, were actually touching the latter's arm when the momentary deceleration occurred as Bridge took over. The sudden slow-down was at a much faster rate than even Lesbee expected. The resistance of space to the forward movement of the ship must be using up more engine power than he had realized; it was taking a lot of thrust to maintain a one gravity acceleration.

The great vessel slowed about 150 miles per hour in the space of a second.

Lesbee took the blow of that deceleration partly against his back, partly against one side—for he had half-turned to defend himself from the bigger man's attack.

Browne, who had nothing to grab on to, was flung forward at the full 150 miles per hour. He struck the control board with an audible thud, stuck to it as if he were glued there; and then, when the adjustment was over—when the *Hope of Man* was again speeding along at one gravity—his body slid down the face of the board, and crumpled into a twisted position on the rubberized dais.

His uniform was discolored. As Lesbee watched, blood seeped through and dripped to the floor.

\*

"Are you going to hold an election?" Tellier asked.

The big ship had turned back under Lesbee's command, and had picked up his friends. The lifeboat itself, with the remaining Karn still aboard, was put into an orbit around Alta III and abandoned.

The two young men were sitting now in the Captain's cabin.

After the question was asked, Lesbee leaned back in his chair, and closed his eyes. He didn't need to examine his total resistance to the suggestion. He had already savored the feeling that command brought.

Almost from the moment of Browne's death, he had observed himself having the same thoughts that Browne had voiced—among many others, the reasons why elections were not advisable aboard a spaceship. He waited now while Eleesa, one of his three wives—she being the younger of the two young widows of Browne—poured wine for them, and went softly out. Then he laughed grimly.

"My good friend," he said, "we're all lucky that time is so compressed at the speed of light. At 500-times compression, any further exploration we do will require only a few months, or years at most. And so I don't think we can afford to take the chance of defeating at an election the only person who understands the details of the new acceleration method. Until I decide exactly how much exploration we shall do, I shall keep our speed capabilities a secret. But I did, and do, think one other person should know where I have this information documented. Naturally, I selected First Officer Tellier."

"Thank you, sir," the youth said. But he was visibly thoughtful as he sipped his wine. He went on finally, "Captain, I think you'd feel a lot better if you held an election. I'm sure you could win it."

Lesbee laughed tolerantly, shook his head. "I'm afraid you don't understand the dynamics of government," he said. "There's no record in history of a person who actually had control, handing it over."

He finished with the casual confidence of absolute power. "I'm not going to be presumptuous enough to fight a precedent like that!"